Building a Fire Truck

Building a Fire Truck

Jerry Bushey

Carolrhoda Books, Inc., Minneapolis

**to my sons, John, Tony, and Matthew,
and to Elmer Abrahamson**

The author wishes to express his gratitude to the General
Safety Equipment Company, especially to Jim Kirvida
and Dick Scheele, for their cooperation and assistance
in producing this book.

LIBRARY OF CONGRESS CATALOGING IN PUBLICATION DATA

Bushey, Jerry.
  Building a fire truck.

  SUMMARY: A step-by-step description of how a single-unit
fire truck is built.

  1. Fire-engines—Juvenile literature. [1. Fire engines] I. Title.

TH9372.B87   628.9′252   81-6182
ISBN 0-87614-170-X   AACR2

2   3   4   5   6   7   8   9   10   87   86   85   84   83

There are about 150 companies in the United States that build fire trucks. This company is the fifteenth largest. Seventy to eighty trucks are built here each year.

Maxi pumper

Pumper

Mini pumper

Snorkel truck

The trucks that are built here are all single-unit trucks. They do not bend in the middle like a hook-and-ladder truck. It takes four to six weeks to build each truck. Four or five trucks are in different stages of being built all the time.

Each truck is custom-built to meet its buyer's own special needs. First the customer chooses the make and engine of the truck. Then the customer buys the cab and frame and has it delivered to the fire truck company.

Pumps ready to be installed

A section of the truck frame is being cut away to make room for the pump.

The fire truck company is now ready to begin work on the truck. First they install a water pump. The water pump will be used to pump water from a fire hydrant or a water tank to the hoses. Every fire truck has a water pump. The pumps are not made at the fire truck company. They are ordered from a company that makes only water pumps. Each pump is ordered specifically for the truck in which it will be installed. It has been built with the exact number of hose outlets that the customer wants and is able to pump the amount of water that the customer needs.

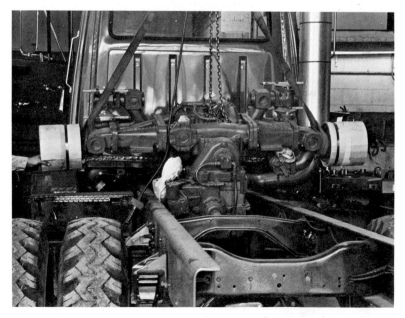

The pump is being lowered into place.

The pump is bolted into place and the drive shaft is hooked up. The drive shaft is the pipe that runs from the front of the truck to the bottom of the pump, then to the back wheels. It makes the water pump work and turns the back wheels.

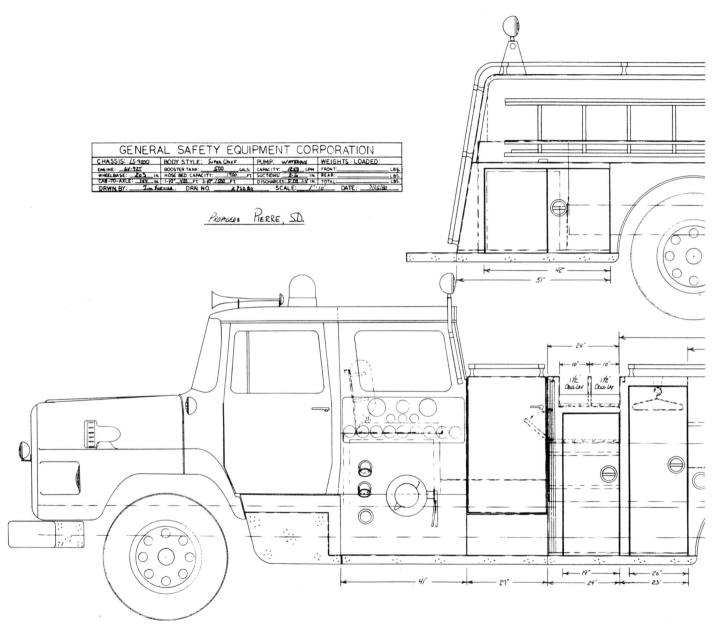

Each fire truck is built according to a set of plans. The plans are drawn up to meet the customer's special needs. Every truck has its own set of plans, and there is a plan for each part of the truck. One truck might have more

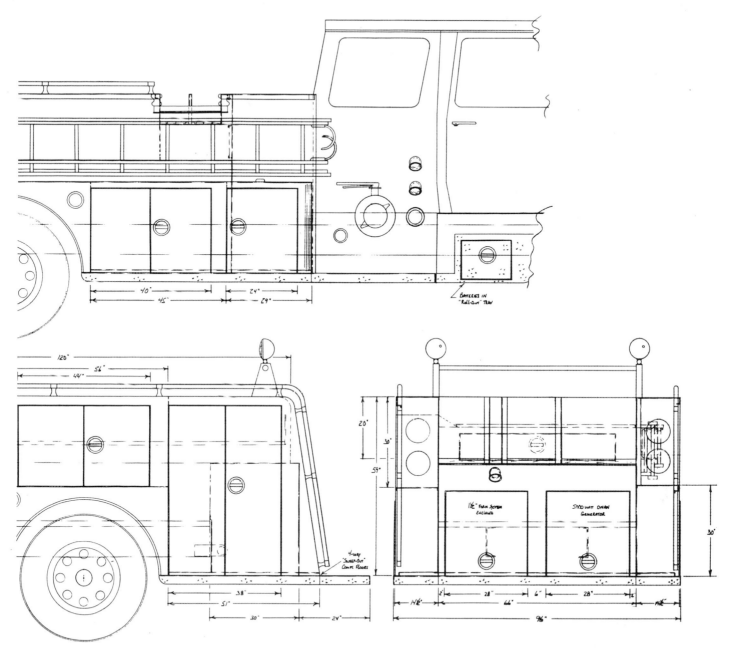

hose outlets than another, or the shape of the body might be different, or it might have more doors and compartments. This plan is for a pumper truck. This part of the plan is for the body.

Before the body can be started, a sub-frame must be built to support it. These pictures show a finished sub-frame for a pumper truck.

Now workers can begin to build the body. The body is like the shell of the truck. It is built from sheets of metal. Each sheet is ⅛ inch thick. That's twice as thick as the metal used for cars.

First the metal must be cut to the right sizes for the different parts of the body. The men below are measuring and cutting the metal.

After a piece of metal has been cut to size, its edges are bent on a machine like the one below. This is done to add strength to the metal and to provide a place where hinges, locks, and bolts can be easily attached.

After the edges have been bent, the corners are welded and ground smooth. This man is grinding the corners of a door.

SAN PEDRO SCHOOL
498 PT. SAN PEDRO ROAD
SAN RAFAEL, CA 94901

Then the parts of the body are bolted together. These side panels are almost ready to be put on a pumper truck. After they have been bolted in place, the water tank will be installed.

Most water tanks hold about 750 gallons of water. The trucks must carry their own water so that some firefighters can start fighting a fire as soon as they get to it, while others are still hooking the truck up to a larger source of water like a hydrant.

The man on the left is finishing a water tank. It will be placed inside the truck above on this side of the panel with the holes in it. The water pump is on the other side of the panel.

This man is standing on the side of the pumper truck. He is making the controls for the valves on the water pump. The valves control which hose the water will go to and how much water will go through the hose.

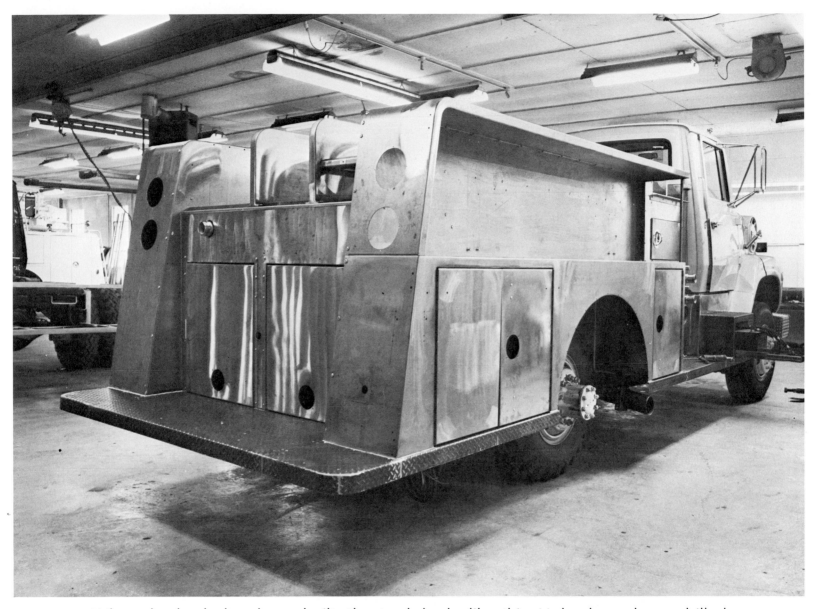

When the body has been built, the truck looks like this. Holes have been drilled for the lights, gauges, and controls. Later on, lights, sirens, railings, gauges, hoses, ladders, and all other moveable parts and parts that need power to be operated will be added to the truck. But first the truck will be painted.

In order for the truck to be painted, it must be taken apart. All the removable parts are taken off. They will be sprayed with enamel paint and then put back on the truck.

The parts that are not removable must also be painted. The areas that will not be painted have been covered with paper and tape. The tires and wheels have been removed, and the truck is sitting on jacks so that some of its undersides can be painted. When everything has been painted, the truck will be put back together.

Now the truck is almost finished, but its tail lights, hose reel, hand rails, dials, and gauges must still be put on.

Gauges

Hose and connection fittings

Ladders

Nozzles

These parts are not made at the fire truck company but by other companies that specialize in making them. The fire truck company orders them in large numbers and in many different sizes so that they will have on hand almost any part a particular fire truck needs.

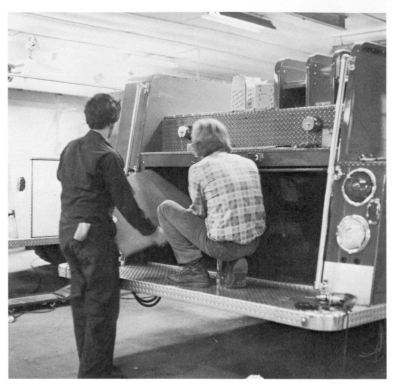

All of these parts are attached
to the truck by hand.

After all the dials and gauges have been put on the control panel, it will look like this. This panel is on the side of the pumper truck. The gauges will tell the firemen how fast the engine is running, how hot it is, how much water the pump is pumping, and how much each hose is spraying. By looking at the gauges the firemen know everything that is happening inside the truck. The controls and some of the hose outlets are also on this panel.

All the missing parts have now been put on this pumper truck. The machine next to the hose is a portable power plant. Sometimes firefighters must use fans to clear smoke out of a building. In a building that has been burning, the electricity is usually out. But fans can be plugged into this portable power plant instead.

Very little has been done to the cab of the fire truck. A short wave radio has been added as well as switches and controls for the lights and sirens.

There is only one thing left to be done: paint the customer's name on the truck. Gold leaf is used for the lettering.

At last the truck is ready to be tested. The company must be certain that everything works properly. Each truck takes six hours to test. A special testing company tests every truck.

This man is checking a gauge to see if the pump is maintaining pressure. It must hold constant pressure for two hours.

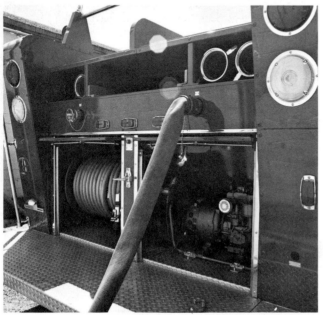

The fire truck company has a large underground water tank. Water for the tests is drawn out of this tank and then sprayed back in so that large amounts of water won't be wasted during the testing.

The large black hose is a suction hose. When the fire truck is on the job, this hose will be attached to a fire hydrant. The pump inside the truck will pull water from the hydrant through this hose to feed the other hoses. This is the only hose that brings water into the truck, so it must be especially strong.

In the picture on the left the foam system is being tested. Foam is used to put out chemical and gas fires.

This pumper truck has been completed, tested, and approved. The customer can now pick it up. Soon it will be used to save people and property from fires. This truck cost about $80,000! Some of the trucks built here cost as much as $250,000!

SAN PEDRO SCHOOL
498 PT. SAN PEDRO ROAD
SAN RAFAEL, CA 94901